# Disney's

# THE KID

Printed in the United States of America.

First Edition
1   3   5   7   9   10   8   6   4   2

This book is set in 11.5-point Bookman.

Library of Congress Catalog Card Number: 00-105969
ISBN: 0-7868-4468-X
For more Disney Press fun, visit www.disneybooks.com

# DISNEY'S

# THE KID

A Junior Novelization by R. M. Gómez

Adapted from the Screenplay Written by Audrey Wells

Produced by Jon Turteltaub,
Christina Steinberg and Hunt Lowry

Directed by Jon Turteltaub

DISNEY PRESS

NEW YORK

# Chapter 1

It was a typically beautiful morning in southern California. Birds were singing, the sun was shining, and light, fluffy clouds sailed across a brilliant blue sky. But Russ Duritz didn't notice any of that. Far below the clouds, inside a sleek convertible on a crowded freeway, Russ tried to squeeze through bumper-to-bumper traffic, talking nonstop to clients on his car phone. As he talked, a fax machine on the dashboard spit out faxes.

"Charlie? It's Russ Duritz. How's Bora Bora? I've got good news for you. You're out of the headlines. *The New York Post* only takes one jab at you in an article on celebrity divorces!"

Russ breezed by a long line of cars waiting for a freeway exit. Then he snuck into the line, nudging his convertible in front of the lead car as the driver slammed on his brakes and yelled, "Jerk!" out the window.

Ignoring the insult, Russ had already switched to his cell phone and was on another call. The work of a high-profile image consultant like Russ was never done. "Hey, Bobby, how are ya? Really? Lunch with the Dalai Lama? No, don't wear that. Wear something more natural—cotton or silk. And leave the Rolex at home!"

Hanging up, he picked up the first phone to give instructions to his assistant: "Janet, terminate the contract with Bobby. When they can't even get dressed without me, it's time to cut the cord!"

Switching to yet another call, Russ did not see the vintage single-prop biplane high above him, soaring through the clouds. In the cockpit was an older man wearing old-fashioned aviator goggles and a helmet. His eyes were focused on Russ's car. He was tailing the convertible from above. Then— suddenly—the pilot took the plane into a steep dive, headed straight for Russ's car!

Russ was so intent on his conversation, however, that he didn't notice—not even when the plane's engine grew so loud that he had to shout to be heard. It wasn't until the plane swooped down and almost gave Russ a haircut that he screamed—"Yaah!"—and nearly lost control of his car. He flinched and dropped his cell phone onto the floor of the car. What in the world was that?

Russ picked up the phone and sat up again. But when he looked up, the plane had disappeared.

Russ searched the sky. Not a sign of anything but clouds and blue sky. And none of the other drivers in the cars around him looked alarmed. Russ turned to the lady sitting next to him in traffic.

"Did you see that?" he asked.

She just gave him a look and rolled up her window. Maybe I'm crazy, Russ thought. After all, who gets buzzed by a propeller plane on the freeway? Maybe he had imagined the whole thing. It was true he had been under a lot of stress lately.

Russ ran his hands through his hair, cleared his throat, and resumed his conversation as if nothing had happened. It was right back to business as usual.

# Chapter 2

**T**hat afternoon at the Los Angeles airport, Russ stopped at a newsstand to pick up some newspapers and entertainment magazines before his flight. Always in a hurry, Russ rushed up to the cashier, but there was a woman in line ahead of him. Russ rolled his eyes as she dug through her many bags, searching for money.

Russ couldn't stand it another second. Over her head, he said to the cashier, "How much is mine?"

"There's someone ahead of you, sir," the cashier responded.

Impatiently, Russ asked, "Well, how much is hers?"

"Five dollars and twenty-six cents," said the cashier.

"Add it to my bill," snapped Russ.

The cashier looked at him and shrugged. She

4

couldn't have cared less who paid for what. "That'll be nineteen sixty-five," she said.

Russ threw a twenty-dollar bill onto the counter and turned to walk away. Taken aback, the woman with the bags called after Russ. "You didn't have to do that for me," she said.

"I *didn't* do it for you," Russ said with a sneer. "Next time, check some bags!"

And with that, Russ breezed off to his gate, while the woman stood there in stunned silence.

The cashier, however, knew the word she was looking for. "Jerk," she said.

One quick airline flight later, Russ walked into the office of Governor Jane Camp and threw down a copy of *Newsweek* magazine. The cover featured her picture, along with the following big headline: "Political Favors for Political Funds."

The governor sat behind her desk, sobbing into a tissue. "It's not my fault it costs eight million dollars to run a campaign in this state," she wailed. "I had a squeaky-clean term in office. I didn't know the contribution was illegal. It's not my job to know!" One of the governor's aides put a hand on her shoulder to comfort her.

Russ stood watching her for a second without saying a word. Then he burst out in a mocking tone, "*Whaa! Whaa!* Somebody call a *whaambulance!*"

Stunned, the governor and her aide stared at Russ.

"What did you say?" the governor asked with a sniffle.

But Russ completely ignored her tears. "Do you know what the number-one killer of politicians under sixty is today?"

Still shocked, she just shook her head no.

"Self-pity," said Russ matter-of-factly. "Self-pity kills. Say it."

"Self-pity kills," the governor repeated.

"Now," Russ continued, "I'll be happy to get you out of this mess. But first you've got to stop crying."

"I'll try."

"No, I mean right now," snapped Russ. "You're giving me a headache."

Obediently, the governor gave one last sniff and reached for another tissue.

Back on the plane and headed for home, Russ tried to get some work done on his laptop. But he was so tired that he just couldn't concentrate. Resting his eyes for a minute, he looked out the window . . . and could not believe what he saw! There in the sky, not twenty feet away, was a single-propeller plane flying right alongside the jet! Russ pressed his face to the window. It was impossible! No propeller plane could fly at that altitude. And it definitely couldn't keep up with a 767. Or fly that close. But there it was!

Or was it? The small plane flew in and out of the clouds. Russ rubbed his eyes and stared harder, trying to get a clear look. Was he seeing things?

And then, a momentary break in the clouds left him with no doubt. There really *was* a small plane flying outside his window. It appeared to have an open cockpit. And the pilot, wearing a flight helmet and goggles, was waving right at Russ! This was the strangest thing he had ever seen. . . .

"Hey! Hey, there." A woman's hand shook Russ lightly by the shoulder and he awoke, startled. He found himself sitting in his airplane seat, next to a blond woman in her forties.

"You were talking in your sleep," she said kindly. She spoke with a strong Southern accent.

Russ shook his head, still waking up. What a weird dream! he thought. He felt his cheek twitch and quickly put up his hand to hide the facial tic. It was the one thing in his life that Russ couldn't manage to control.

He apologized to his seatmate. "Sorry, just a . . . dream I've been having lately."

She smiled and gave Russ a sympathetic look. "Want to tell me about it?" she asked. "Poor thing. You're under a lot of stress. What kind of work do you do?"

Ugh! thought Russ. Just what he hated most—a chatty seatmate! He tried to turn her off. "It's hard to explain what I do," he said shortly.

"Oh," she answered, now even more interested. "Must be something with the Internet? Or finance? Or genetic engineering?"

Russ rolled his eyes. "I'm an image consultant, okay?" He turned to his laptop, trying to go back to work. But the woman wouldn't quit. She had no idea who she was messing with!

"An image consultant?" she continued, her face brightening. "So you kinda troubleshoot for folks— give 'em makeovers when they need some revamping, right?"

"Yes," Russ answered gruffly. "And you're not going to shut up until we get to Los Angeles, are you?"

For a moment, the woman looked stunned. Then her smile returned. "Right," she said playfully.

"Wrong," Russ answered. "Because I'm not too polite to tell you, 'I'm tired, you're boring, and I'm really not interested in you.'" With that, he returned to his work.

The woman smiled to herself and shook her head. "Jerk," she said to Russ, and then calmly flipped through her magazine.

Now Russ was the stunned one. "Excuse me?" he asked, turning to her again.

"I said you're a jerk," she answered. "This can't be the first time you've heard that."

She had that right. It wasn't even the first time that day! "You're right," said Russ. "People call me that left and right. They run screaming down the street!"

The woman laughed. Then she said, "Look, my name's Deirdre. I'm flying into L.A. to start an anchor job at the local news and I think I sat next to you for a reason. I think you're supposed to give me a little image consulting."

Russ thought that over for a minute. He had to admire her nerve. "Okay," he said. "If I do this, will you be quiet the rest of the flight?"

"Quiet as the dead," Deirdre answered.

Russ sighed, and then began to study her from head to toe. He figured he might as well get this over with. "Your hair's too big, your brows are too dark, your nails are too long, and your makeup is too orange. Your perfume is too sweet, your heels are too high, and your jewelry is too cheap."

"What about my accent?" Deirdre asked, not

looking the least bit insulted. "Everyone's warned me to stop saying 'y'all.'"

"Don't ever stop saying 'y'all,'" Russ told her. "Your 'y'all' is your trademark. Say 'y'all' and you'll be promoted within six months. Say 'y'all' with a smile and you'll be famous in twelve."

"Thank you!" Deirdre said with a huge smile.

"You're welcome," Russ answered. "Now will you please shut up so I can get back to work?"

Russ and Deirdre smirked at each other for a moment. Then Russ turned back to the window. There was absolutely no sign of the propeller plane. That was a really strange dream, he thought with a chuckle.

# Chapter 3

It was after dark by the time Russ drove up to his house in Hollywood Hills, exhausted from the long day. Glad to be home, Russ steered into his driveway, and was startled when a small figure darted in front of his car. He slammed on the brakes as it ran into the bushes and disappeared. What, or who, was that? Russ wondered.

Shaken, Russ went inside, changed into his pajamas, and started his nightly ritual: mixing a package of powdered vitamins into a glass of water. Then he picked up the phone and dialed Janet's number as he furiously mixed the green water.

"There is no way *anybody* should get past my gate!" Russ fumed over the phone. "Call the alarm company right now. I want the sensitivity set on ten. I want to see the Fourth of July around here the minute anyone steps on my property. Write that down, Janet!"

"Okay, I got that," Janet answered sleepily. It was after midnight. She and her husband had been fast asleep before Russ's call. "It was probably just some neighborhood kid."

But Russ rambled on to Janet as he listened to the messages on his answering machine. "I want Rottweilers. I want the guy who trained the Rottweilers to be afraid to come here. I want a moat with lava in it!"

He sped through the first message from a woman with a sultry voice. He stopped it several times, only to hear her yell "jerk"—"jerk"—"jerk"—"jerk" each time.

The next message was left by an older man with a gravelly voice. "Russ, it's Dad," said the voice. "I'm calling to remind you that I'm moving next Sunday and I hope you're going to give me a hand."

Russ paused the machine for a second and spoke into the phone to Janet. "Number one on your to-do list: messenger my father a check for one thousand dollars and a note explaining that he should use the money to hire movers, as I am busy on Sunday and cannot help him myself."

When he hit the play button again, his father's voice went on: "You should come over and go through the boxes in the attic. I found some of your old things up there . . ." Russ immediately deleted the rest of the message. He grabbed some faxes from his machine and made his way up the stairs to his bedroom, still on the phone with Janet.

"I have the schedule you faxed me," he said, "and I want to take the first five calls from home tomorrow, starting with the Larry King conference call at six A.M. I will save Bob Riley from the firing squad. I will meet him at the stadium tomorrow at three P.M. I'll need twelve cream pies and Amy Henley—make sure they're all at the owner's box by two-forty-five. I'm getting into bed now and I do not want to talk to you or anybody else until I go back to work in four hours."

"Guess what?" Janet snapped. "Neither do I!"

She hung up on Russ as her husband Harry rolled over and mumbled, "Jerk." Janet sighed and turned off the light.

Just as he did every night, Russ settled into bed with the TV on for company. The remote was cradled on his pillow. He switched off the light and closed his eyes. Only seconds later, Russ was sitting straight up in bed, listening to a scuffling sound outside his house. Remembering the figure in the driveway earlier, he turned the light back on, jumped out of bed, and moved into his living room. He peeked out into the garden and watched, but he couldn't see anything stirring. Then, just as he was about to turn and go back to bed, he spotted a shadow—a small object sitting on his front steps. But he couldn't quite make out what it was.

He deactivated his house alarm and opened the front door. What is this? Russ wondered, picking up a small wooden airplane at his feet. Feeling very nervous, Russ peered out into the darkness, shut the door, and reactivated the alarm. Then he looked down at the toy plane and turned it over in his hands. Underneath one of the wings, the toy was marked with a name: "Rusty."

Russ thought for a minute, puzzled. Then he shook his head, remembering the message from his father about his things in the attic. "Dad, you're getting weird!" he said out loud. He set the plane down on a table and headed off to bed.

# Chapter 4

"**W**hat *happened* to you?" Janet asked Russ when he strode into the office the next morning. He looked exhausted.

"Nothing," Russ answered. "I just didn't get my beauty sleep."

"No kidding," said Janet. "Well, there's somebody waiting for you in your office."

"Who?" Russ asked. Through an inner window, Russ could see his father standing awkwardly in his office, waiting for him.

Right away, Russ's cheek began to twitch. Then he launched into business mode. "Okay, Janet, here's what I need you to do. Wait sixty seconds. Then come in and tell me that I'm late for something."

"Fight fair," Janet called to her boss as he headed into his office.

Sam Duritz was standing in front of a bookshelf looking at a framed photo when Russ walked in.

"Nice photo of you with Al De Niro," Sam said.

"*Robert* De Niro," Russ corrected him.

"Nice photo of you with Robert De Niro," said Sam, trying again.

"Thanks," said Russ. "But that's Al Pacino."

"Too bad," Sam answered sarcastically.

Already, Russ and his dad were bickering. Russ went to his computer and started checking his E-mail. "So what can I do for you, Dad?" he asked. "Didn't you get the check I sent this morning?"

"I did," his father said, pulling the check out of his pocket. "But I didn't ask for a check. I asked you to come over and help me lift a few things. Or is writing a check the only manual labor you do?" Even before the words were out of his mouth, Sam wished he could take back that last part.

Russ rolled with the punches. "Time is money," he said flatly. "And my time costs a lot more than a mover's. I'm afraid a check is all that I can afford."

Sam sighed and dropped the check on his son's desk. He wished he could walk out, come back in, and start over. "Your sister and her family are coming over for dinner tomorrow. You haven't seen your niece and nephew in a long time . . . and you might want some of those things in the attic."

Russ was working away at his desk. "What would I want, Dad? More model airplanes?" He looked up at his father. "Tell me, how many times in the twenty years you've lived in that house have I wanted anything? Anything at all?"

Father and son stared at each other. The office was silent.

Just then, Janet opened the door and announced to Russ, "You're late for a very big meeting. Dozens of irate and highly important people are clamoring for you. There's pandemonium, I'm sure, somewhere. And you really must go right now."

Russ logged off his computer and got up to leave. "Dad, good luck with the move. Let me know how it goes." Without looking back, he headed out the door.

When he was gone, Janet looked over at Sam. "He's a stubborn one," she said.

"Wonder where he got that from," Sam said sarcastically.

Right on time for his three o'clock appointment at the baseball stadium, Russ wove his way through a crowd of fans, heading for the owner's box. As he rounded a corner, he came upon Amy Henley, his partner and a professional photographer. Amy had

**17**

her digital camera out and was taking pictures of a fat hot dog vendor.

"Signed a new client?" joked Russ, as he walked over to Amy's side.

Amy barely cracked a smile at the sight of Russ. "We made a bet," she said. "I make him look heroic, I get a free hot dog."

Russ looked the vendor over from head to toe. "You're going to starve," he announced to Amy.

"Not a chance," Amy answered, with a gleam in her eye. Russ had a way of getting under Amy's skin. But she knew how to dish it out to him, too.

Russ went over to the vendor. "Suck it in, big boy," he instructed the man.

"Hey, leave the belly alone. I like the belly," said Amy.

Russ smirked. "Bellies like that are only good if your name is Buddha!" The vendor sucked in his gut and struck a pose.

"Oooo, lovely!" said Amy.

"Take the shot now," said Russ.

"Stop bossing!" Amy replied.

They stared at each other for a moment, then Amy snapped the shutter on the digital camera. Together, Russ and Amy checked the image, then showed it to the hot dog man.

"Poetry," announced Russ.

"Nice," said the vendor, pleased with the result. "Here's your hot dog. Just don't share it with jerko," he said, gesturing at Russ.

As they rushed up toward the owner's box, Russ took the hot dog from Amy's hand and tossed it right into the trash.

"Hey! I worked hard for that!" said Amy. Only ten minutes, and already she had had just about enough of Russ for one day.

"You shouldn't eat that junk," said Russ. "And stop biting your nails!"

"I don't bite my nails," Amy argued. "I bite only one nail. And why do you care?"

They reached the owner's box and told the security guard who they were. As they waited to be admitted, Amy grabbed Russ's arm and said, "Wait a minute!"

Russ gave her an impatient look. "What is it now?"

"Hi," she said.

"Hi," Russ answered.

Amy smiled at him. "We haven't seen each other in a couple of days. How have you been?"

"Fine. *Now* can we go in?" Russ asked.

"No," Amy said. "Now's the part where you ask me." She sounded like a teacher instructing a small child.

Russ rolled his eyes. "You're just trying to

humanize me again," he complained.

"I know," Amy said. "And I'm sure I'm wasting my time!"

Russ cracked a smile, and they entered the box.

As soon as Bob Riley, the team's owner, saw Russ and Amy, he shouted, "Hey! Russ Duritz to the rescue! Here to save my sorry butt! Get him a drink. He's going to need it!"

A young man, Mr. Riley's assistant, came over and introduced himself to Amy and Russ. "I'm Josh. If you need anything—"

"I do," Russ interrupted, springing into action. "Go up to the cheap seats. Find me a dozen eight- to twelve-year-olds. Eight boys, four girls, four white, five black, three Latino. Bring 'em back in three minutes."

As Josh rushed off, Russ asked Amy to set up her camera equipment. Then he settled down to talk with Bob.

"So why is everybody busting my chops?" Bob wanted to know. "The way I see this thing, it's just a misunderstanding!" Bob said.

Russ looked thoughtful. Then he said sarcastically, "Well, let me see if I can explain to you how other people 'see this thing.' See, to Joe Baseball Fan out there, you're the guy who promised five percent of every ticket sold this season would go toward establishing a baseball camp for inner-city kids. And you're the guy who released pictures to the press of kids attending that baseball camp, which, in fact, *does not exist!*"

Right away, Bob was on the defensive. "I was gonna get around to it eventually. So it slipped my mind for a while. I'm a busy guy. What are they gonna do, yell at me?"

"No, Bob," Russ replied. "You're not a busy guy, you're a *stupid* guy. You decided to play Mr. Charitable so that the city council would build you a brand-new ballpark. Now you look like a big fat liar who stole from kids. Good-bye, new ballpark. Hello, jail."

Bob squirmed in his chair. "So what's your big plan?" he asked Russ hopefully.

Russ rubbed his hands together. "First off," he began, "you're going to pick up the phone, call your accountants, and tell them to deposit a check into the ball camp fund *today*. Second, you're going to explain how that picture you distributed was 'intentionally staged for fund-raising purposes only.' And lastly, how do you like chocolate cream pie?"

Just then, Josh came in with the twelve kids Russ had asked for.

Bob looked confused. "Why?" he asked. "You're

gonna feed the kids cream pie to get me out of this mess?"

"No," Russ corrected him. "The kids are going to feed *you* cream pie and get you out of this mess. Prepare to be . . . pied! Amy, is that a word?"

"Yes, I believe that's correct," Amy answered as she handed out pies. "'To pie' somebody. I pie, you pie, he/she/it pies. You'd find that in the newer dictionaries."

"Hey!" Bob protested, starting to look uncomfortable.

"Listen, Bob," Russ said. "When a rich guy gets a pie in the face, it makes the evening news. And that's what you want, to be all over the news as quickly as possible. You need to make a joke out of this mess before you spend the rest of your life in court. You need to make a public apology that is humorous and very, very humiliating."

Bob looked hard at Russ. Finally, he sighed and started to take off his jacket. "Okay, pie me," he said. Then, pointing at Russ, he said, "Jerk."

Later that evening, Russ and Amy relaxed over dinner at a sushi bar. They were just about the last customers left in the place. Takeshi, the sushi chef, was working away behind the counter.

"Tell me, Takeshi," Russ asked him. "If you get

called a jerk four times in one day, does that mean it's true?"

"Only four?" said Amy with mock surprise. "Did you get up late?"

"I'm *asking* Tak," Russ said firmly.

Tak thought it over and said, "Four times *is* a pattern. But it takes five to make it fact."

"Then there's hope!" Russ said.

"Jerk," said Amy.

Russ looked at Amy. She had seemed to be in a bad mood all evening. "Are you okay?" he asked her.

"Oh, I'm *just* fine," Amy said sarcastically. "I was just sitting here thinking about the great campaign we could do for Hitler. Or Saddam Hussein. We could get a bunch of cute, little furry animals to sing a little tune supporting chemical warfare. We could really overturn his image problem."

Russ laughed, thinking it was a joke. "O-kay," he said.

Amy went on: "Or a television special with a guest appearance by Satan. Now there's a fellow who's always been misunderstood! What if we get him out of that depressing red devil suit and into something a little breezier? Then we could have him do a tap dance routine with . . . Frankenstein's monster! *He's* due for a makeover.

**23**

We get a hat to cover that flat head, maybe a nice tie to cover the electrodes. I mean, that's really *your* area, but . . ."

Now Russ was starting to get the picture. "Amy, please," he said, interrupting her. "I'm going to edit this afternoon's tape very carefully. And there's nothing wrong with doing the right thing for our client, Bob Riley. He pays me . . . us . . . a lot of money to do what we do."

"Well, he's a stinky man in a stinky mess," Amy continued. "I'm thinking that we're too old for this."

"Too old for what?" Russ asked.

"Too old to be apologizing for idiot creeps like Bob Riley," she replied.

Russ did not seem moved at all. "Are you going to finish that?" Russ asked, reaching for some sushi on Amy's plate.

"You should be concerned about this," Amy said, looking at Russ seriously. "You're the one turning forty on Thursday."

"Thank you for reminding me," Russ complained. He knew he wasn't getting any younger, and he was very aware of his upcoming birthday.

"Look, Russ," Amy went on. "I don't expect any of this to sway you. It's just that we can't go around talking about what we're going to be like when we grow up. We are up. Two years ago when

I signed on with you, it was different. But today we shamelessly exploited innocent children—simply to help a creep with his cash-flow problems."

Something on Russ's face made Amy wonder if she was getting to him, even just a little bit. "Is that it?" Russ asked.

"Yes," said Amy.

"Check, please," Russ said. Suddenly, without warning, he stood up, grabbed the tape of Bob Riley and the kids, and threw it across the restaurant. It landed with a clank inside the waiter's bus tray.

Amy froze. She was absolutely stunned; so stunned that it took her a few minutes to collect herself and follow Russ out of the sushi bar. "I can't believe you *did* that," she said, laughing. "It was fantastic!"

The waiter had already come outside to empty the trash. As Russ lingered by the Dumpster, Amy could read the look on his face. She held him back. "You are *not* going Dumpster diving to look for that smelly, fish-encrusted tape."

"You're right," said Russ. "My suit cost two grand. Let me give *you* a boost."

Amy dragged him away and tried to distract him. "Look at the moon," she said.

"*Look at the moon?*" Russ asked in a mocking tone.

Amy nodded. "It's beautiful . . . it's big . . . it's revolving around the earth. Proving once again that the universe does not revolve around you. You looking?"

"I looked," said Russ. Amy was irritating him. "Let me show you something, Amy. Tell me if this is cute." He started to imitate Amy: *"Look at the moon. Ooooh! It's so big. And look at me! I'm so perky when I get excited about the moon, no one would ever know I'm almost thirty!"* Russ dropped the girly voice and looked at Amy. "What do you think? Cute? Or just stupid?"

Russ's rudeness shocked Amy so much that she couldn't say anything for a minute. Then finally she took a deep breath and said, "Listen, I'm telling you, if you don't start being a little nicer to people, you're going to end up old and alone. Sometimes I don't know how I can stand you another second. But then, just when I'm about to quit, you do something—like tonight when you threw that tape away—and I catch the tiniest, briefest glimpse of the kid in you. And that's when I decide to hang in there for five more minutes and see what happens next. Good night."

Russ watched her leave, a strange expression on his face. Had he been too hard on her? he wondered. His conscience troubled him a second, but then he shook off the thought and strolled away.

That night, Russ was fast asleep in bed when a loud crash woke him. Grabbing a baseball bat for a weapon, Russ tiptoed down the hallway toward the kitchen where the noises were coming from. Peering through the darkness, he could just make out a shadow standing in the kitchen sink, struggling to open the window! Russ reached for the light switch, flipped it on, and saw . . . a small boy!

"Hey!" Russ shouted in alarm.

The boy turned around, trembling with fear. In his hands, he was clutching the model airplane that Russ had found on his doorstep the other night.

"What are you doing?" Russ demanded.

Suddenly, the terrified boy dropped the plane into the sink and dove headfirst out the kitchen window.

But Russ was too quick for the boy. He rushed forward and grabbed the boy's legs just as they were about to disappear through the window. Desperate to get away, the boy kicked and flailed his legs until—*bam!*—a sneakered foot kicked Russ right in the head.

Russ reeled back, slightly stunned, and let go. The kid fell out the window with a *thud* and a loud "Owww!"

Russ poked his head out the window to see him trying to recover from the bad fall. "Are you okay?" Russ asked him.

As the boy scrambled to his feet, Russ finally got a good look at him. He was pudgy and geeky-looking, probably about 8 years old. As he and Russ stared at each other, Russ began to have the strangest feeling that he'd seen this kid before. But before he could put his finger on it, the kid suddenly turned and ran for his bike.

Oh, no, thought Russ. He was going to get to the bottom of this. In hot pursuit, Russ rushed out of his house, hopped into his car, and took off after the kid, who was pedaling away on his bike as fast as he could. He chased the kid through alleys and parking lots, but the kid found shortcuts and kept getting away from him. At last, Russ was sure he had him. He chased him down a narrow passage between two large buildings. There seemed to be nowhere the kid could go, but he turned a corner. Russ followed him out into the clearing and almost had his head taken off. A small propeller plane came out of nowhere and narrowly missed Russ.

What is going on? thought Russ. He was definitely having some strange run-ins with airplanes

Russ was so intent on his conversation that he didn't notice the plane—not even when its engine grew so loud that he had to shout to be heard.

"Don't ever stop saying 'y'all,'" Russ told Deirdre. "Your 'y'all' is your trademark."

Bob Riley sighed and took off his jacket. "Okay, pie me," he said.

"If you don't start being a little nicer to people, you're going to end up old and alone," said Amy.

"You are having these hallucinations for a reason," Dr. Alexander said.

The kid picked up the plane, looked underneath, and pointed to the name written there.

"You can . . . um . . . see him?" Russ asked.
"Yes . . . um . . . I can," said Janet.

"Suddenly I am in touch with my magic assistant powers,"
Janet yelled. "Shazam! Kalamazoo! Poof-a-rama! Zap!"

"What *did* you come for?" asked Russ.
"I dunno," answered Rusty.

The bell rang—*clang!*—and Russ and Rusty started dancing around each other in the ring.

Amy reached out and lifted the hair off Rusty's neck. She found the same mole that was on Russ's neck!

As the kid passed the row where Amy and Russ were sitting, Russ caught his eye and clearly mouthed the words "Don't trip!"

"Amy?" said Rusty. "I have a question. A big one."

Russ did not have much time to tell the kid what was about to happen.

Russ looked seriously at Rusty and said, "I won't let you down anymore."

Russ lifted his arms to the sky and cried, "I . . . am . . . not . . . a . . . *loser*!"

lately. Russ looked around and realized that he was on the runway of a small airfield for private planes. Ahead of him, the kid had already ditched his bike and run into the small airport coffee shop. Russ jumped out of his car and chased after him.

Russ ran into the coffee shop, mildly surprised that it was still open that late. Looking around, he saw that it was filled with senior citizens, whose conversations halted when he came through the door.

"Uh . . . good evening," Russ said to them. "A kid ran in here. Just a moment ago. Did any of you see anything?" When there was no answer from the customers, Russ added, "*Can* any of you see anything?"

The people shrugged and turned away, getting back to their conversations.

Russ walked up and down a row of booths, searching for the boy. "Because I saw this kid— who broke into my house—just run in here . . ."

Russ hopped onto the counter and glanced behind it. Nothing.

" . . . and I could swear he's around here somewhere . . ." Russ went on.

He looked in the kitchen. No kid. Just then he heard the scrape of a chair as someone got up to leave. Russ turned just in time to see a policeman headed out the door. "Hey, Officer? Officer!" called Russ. "Could you hold on? Could I ask you something?"

The officer kept walking without looking back. Russ followed, pushing through the door right behind him and found himself back outside . . . alone. What? Where was the policeman? Russ blinked. There was his car. There was the airport. But the policeman was gone. The kid was gone. And, what was even weirder—Russ whirled around—the coffee shop was gone! He rubbed his eyes. He turned around again. Have I gone insane? Russ asked himself. Shaken, he felt his knees give way as he sank down onto the ground.

"Uh-oh," he said. What was happening to him? Russ wondered if it was time to talk to someone.

# Chapter 5

**T**he next morning, Russ was pacing back and forth in the office of Dr. Alexander, a thoughtful-looking female psychologist. "I'd like to get right to the point, Doctor," Russ said. "I have to be in a meeting in ten minutes."

"You're entitled to a fifty-minute hour," said Dr. Alexander.

"I only need a five-minute hour," Russ assured her. "Or however long it takes you to write out a prescription."

"I see," said the doctor, squinting at Russ. "And what do you need a prescription for?"

"I don't want to talk about it," Russ said. "And I don't want to be in therapy."

"Well, why are you here?" Dr. Alexander asked.

"Why?" Russ repeated. He couldn't figure out

how to explain that one. He thought it over until, finally, he exploded. "You know what the number-one killer of professional men under forty is? Self-pity. I hate talking about myself. It's stupid. I've forgotten about my childhood and I'd like to keep it that way. Just shut up and leave it in the past."

Dr. Alexander let Russ vent. Then she said, "But it doesn't want to stay in the past, does it? Why don't you just sit down and help me understand the issues."

"Issue," Russ corrected her, holding up one finger. "Singular. I have one issue." Russ looked very uncomfortable as he got ready to blurt it out. "I'm . . . seeing things. For the last few weeks, I've been seeing a guy in a plane. And I guess it's getting worse, because now I'm also seeing a kid. A kid who . . . seems a little familiar to me."

"How?" asked the doctor.

"That's none of your business!" snapped Russ.

"Excuse me," said Dr. Alexander, "but this visit is to help you!"

Russ was obviously very upset. This whole thing was taking its toll and getting in the way of his work and his life. A twitching attack overtook his eye. He tried to control it as he told the doctor, "Look, the deal on the table is this: you give me a prescription in the next sixty seconds that will help me *today* or I'm out of here for good."

The doctor looked at Russ and said, "Mr. Duritz, I notice that your eye is twitching."

"I don't have a tic!" shouted Russ.

"I didn't say you had a tic," the doctor said soothingly.

"Well, I don't have a tic!" Russ repeated. "I don't have an ulcer. I don't have a drinking problem. I don't have a smoking problem. What I *do* have are hallucinations, which is why I would really like to leave here—right now—with a prescription I can pick up on my way to work."

The doctor hesitated. Russ smiled charmingly. Finally, Dr. Alexander gave in and wrote out a prescription. She tore it off and handed it to Russ. "You will pick up your prescription and then you will go home and take the rest of the day off. It's for a total of four pills. They will keep you calm until four o'clock tomorrow. I expect to see you back here then." The doctor gave Russ a serious, stern look. "You are having these hallucinations for a reason, and you need to figure out what that reason is."

"Yes, ma'am." Russ grabbed the prescription from her hand and dashed out the door.

• • •

Back at home, Russ switched on the television to watch one of his clients on *Larry King Live*. As he watched, he called Janet on his cell phone and made himself a big bowl of popcorn.

"What's he doing?" he complained to Janet. "He's not sticking to our script! He's making himself look like an idiot!"

"He's an actor," Janet said. "He's improvising."

Russ put down the popcorn and turned up the TV volume. Then he headed into the kitchen to make himself a sandwich. As he hung up with Janet, he suddenly heard a children's cartoon blasting from his television set. What had happened to Larry King? Russ froze for a moment, not sure if his ears were playing tricks on him. After the past few days' events, he couldn't be too sure.

Russ slowly peeked back around the corner into the living room. Sure enough, the channel had changed. And that wasn't all. Russ's chair was swiveling slightly. And the popcorn was gone. As he slowly approached his chair from behind, he thought he could hear a crunching sound. He reached out cautiously for the chair, then whirled it around quickly to see . . . the kid! The kid from the kitchen sink . . . the same kid who had disappeared at the airfield!

"Ahhh!" screamed the kid, dropping popcorn all over himself.

"You!" shouted Russ. "Look. This is not going to work. You can't break into people's homes. What I'm gonna do right now is to call the police and ask them to . . ."

Russ trailed off as the feeling of familiarity about this boy almost overpowered him. "Do I know you?" he asked.

"I don't know," said the kid with a shrug.

Russ grabbed the remote control and turned off the TV. He swallowed hard, staring at the kid. The boy's eyes were the same color as Russ's. He had a bowl haircut and pants that showed three inches of sock.

"Why do you keep coming back here?" Russ asked the kid.

"I just came back to get my airplane, and then . . . I saw the popcorn," the kid said sheepishly. Russ noticed that he spoke with a lisp.

"*Your* plane?" asked Russ.

The kid reached for the model plane. "Yes, my plane. My mom gave it to me for Christmas. How'd *you* get it?"

Russ wrinkled his face and said, "What are you talking about? My dad just sent it over here. It was in his attic. That plane's been mine for thirty . . . *years.*"

The kid picked up the plane, looked under the wing, and pointed to the name written there. "Then why does it have my name on it? Look, right here. It says 'Rusty.'"

Russ looked sick. The kid still didn't get it.

Russ said, "Rusty? Russel Morley Duritz?"

"I hate that stupid name," said the kid. "Hey, wait a minute. How do you know my name?"

Russ continued with a twinge of fear in his voice, "Your mother's name is Gloria. Your father's name is Sam."

"How do you know all that?" the kid asked.

"And your sister's name is Joanne . . ." Russ said.

The kid said, "But everybody calls her . . ."

"Josie," said the two of them together.

Russ and Rusty stared at each other. Slowly the kid was beginning to figure out what was going on. At that moment, they both scratched their right temples with the same finger. They looked each other up and down. They both pulled up their left pant legs to reveal identical scars on their shins. Next, they pulled their shirt collars down. They both had matching moles just above their collarbones. Finally, Rusty held up his hand and wiggled his fingers in the air, making his knuckles crack. Russ did the same.

"Are you who I think you are?" Rusty asked Russ.

"I don't know," answered Russ.

"How did I get here?" asked the kid.

Russ had the same answer: "I don't know." He was completely stunned. The two of them had the same names, same scars, same moles, same eyes. The reason Rusty looked so familiar to Russ was because he reminded him . . . of himself! Himself as a kid!

"How old are you?" asked Rusty.

"Forty . . . in a couple of days," said Russ.

"Wow. That's *old*," remarked the kid. "I'm only eight. This is scary."

Suddenly, Russ started to chuckle. Then his chuckle turned into a laugh—a hysterical laugh. "No, this is not scary. It's . . . hilarious! It's finally happened. I'm finally having a nervous breakdown, and it's not as bad as I thought it would be! I'm just going to close my eyes, and when I open them, he'll be gone."

Russ opened his eyes to find Rusty still staring at him. He walked back into the kitchen, trying not to hyperventilate. "I am a man in my kitchen. I am a man in my kitchen . . . making a sandwich." He started to make a crazy sandwich, grabbing anything he could find nearby and throwing it onto the bread. "It's funny that I hallucinated he knew we called Joanne Josie, but I'm the only one who had a nickname for Aunt Cathy when she had her epileptic spells . . ."

"Aunt Spazzy!" Rusty called in from the living room.

Russ froze for a moment. The kid was right! Russ went back to his sandwich. "I am making a sandwich. The sandwich is real. Focus on the sandwich."

When Rusty came into the kitchen and offered Russ a jar of mustard, Russ jumped with fright. So did the kid. "Am I having a nightmare?" Rusty asked.

"No, *you're* not having a nightmare. *I'm* having a nightmare. You don't exist. I'm having my first nervous breakdown and I'm not sure how they work, but I think I'm dreaming," Russ said. "I'm dreaming, *dreaming*, DREAMING!"

"I don't think you're dreaming," Rusty said, "'cause you're talking and your eye is sort of twitching."

Russ put his hand up to his face to stop the tic. Just then it occurred to him that the twitch was the only characteristic of his that the kid *didn't* have.

Suddenly, Russ turned to face Rusty, pointed a

finger at him, and shouted, "Listen up! I don't have time to go crazy. If you want me to go crazy, you have to go through my office and schedule it through Janet, just like everybody else!"

Rusty just stared at Russ. "Will you make me a sandwich?" he asked.

Russ grabbed his sandwich and rushed up the stairs to his bedroom. "I'm going upstairs to return my calls. Going to contact the outside world. I'm going to return my calls. Going to contact the outside world." He grabbed his phone and dialed Janet's number. "Hi, Janet. It's Russ. I'm upstairs returning my calls. I was downstairs, now I'm upstairs."

Suddenly, Rusty appeared next to his bed, holding out a tomato slice. "You dropped this," he said.

"Ahhh!" Russ screamed as he slammed down the phone. He took his sandwich and rushed into his bathroom, locking the door behind him. In the bathroom, he grabbed the bottle of medicine that Dr. Alexander had prescribed and announced to Rusty, through the door, "You are just a hallucination. I am taking a very powerful medicine, which is going to make you disappear. Prepare to disappear." When the kid didn't answer, Russ continued, "I am sitting on the floor waiting for the very powerful medicine to kick in." Still no answer from Rusty.

"Disappeared?" asked Russ through the door. He crawled to the bathroom door, still holding his sandwich. Then he unlocked the door and opened it to find the kid sitting cross-legged on the floor. He looked sad as he announced, "I'm still here."

Russ stared at him for a minute, stumped. Then he snapped his fingers and said, "We'll just see about that! Come on."

Just as he had asked, Janet came to meet Russ in the underground parking garage at his office. Russ appeared from behind a post and walked over to her.

Without any greeting, Russ said, "Listen, remember the confidentiality papers you signed? If you *ever* talk to anyone about anything from this office, I will sue you and put you in financial ruin."

Unimpressed, Janet said, "Snore."

"Okay, then," Russ said. He whistled, and Rusty appeared from behind the same post. Meekly, he walked over to Russ and Janet.

Janet looked from Rusty to Russ and back again. Then she gave Russ a look that said, "So?"

"You can . . . um . . . see him?" Russ asked.

"Yes . . . um . . . I can," said Janet.

"You can. Okay." Russ sighed, feeling relieved about that much. "This boy is me. At age eight. I

**40**

want you to make him disappear."

Janet looked at Russ curiously. "How was the therapist this morning?"

"Just do it!" shouted Russ.

"How?" shouted Janet, looking bewildered.

"*You're* the assistant," Russ said. "You figure it out!"

Janet had just about had it. "Oh, you yelled at me! Great! That's so helpful! Suddenly I am in touch with my magic assistant powers," she yelled. "Shazam! Kalamazoo! Poof-a-rama! Zap!"

Rusty stared at her, terrified. What was the deal with this lady?

"Rats," said Janet, pretending to be surprised that it didn't work.

"I'm extremely disappointed in you, Janet," said Russ.

"I'm fired, I hope," she said in reply.

"No chance," said Russ. "But you can forget about your bonus."

"Boo-hoo," said Janet. "Where's my dental plan?"

As Russ motioned for the kid to get back in the car, Janet leaned down to Rusty and said, "My boss appears to have lost his mind. Sure you wouldn't rather stay here with me?"

"I'll be okay," Rusty replied.

Janet watched Russ peel out in his car and speed away with the kid. "I hope so," she said.

Russ sped through the city streets. Rusty sniffled and wiped his eyes. "You're going too fast," he complained.

"*Whaa! Whaa!*" Russ responded in his mocking crybaby tone. "Somebody call the *whaambulance*! How am I going to get rid of you?"

"Just take me home," said Rusty.

Hmm, thought Russ. Why hadn't he thought of that?

# Chapter 6

"**R**emind me where you live," Russ said to Rusty.

"You should know that," he answered.

"Well, I don't," said Russ. "We moved about a dozen times."

"A dozen times?" asked the kid, surprised to hear what the future held. "How did that happen?"

Russ answered impatiently. "A big truck comes, you put all your stuff inside, you move to a new house. Twelve times."

Just then, Rusty spotted his house. "That's it, right over there. Remember it?"

There was *something* about the house—something that made Russ slightly uneasy. But he said, "No, I don't remember it."

The kid pointed. "Look. That's where we fell off the roof last year. That's the bush we fell into.

There's where that really big possum crawled under the house. Remember?"

"Sorry, kid," Russ snapped. "I don't remember the possum. I hardly remember living here at all. But you do. Bye, now."

"Wait," Rusty said, looking more closely. "The house. It's different."

As they sat parked outside, an Asian American family came out of the front door and climbed into a car in the driveway.

"Who are *they*?" Rusty asked.

"I should have known this wasn't going to work!" exclaimed Russ, dropping his head into his hands. Obviously, there was another family now living in the house that used to be Rusty's.

The kid started sniffling and crying. What was he going to do now? In response, Russ said, "You know what the number-one killer of boys under ten is? Self-pity. And you're pitiful enough as it is!"

Rusty struck back. "Well, at least I don't do this," he said, imitating Russ's facial twitch. Now Russ was *really* mad.

Russ entered the front door of his house with Rusty right on his heels. As Russ slumped into a chair, Rusty wandered through the house, shouting, "Chester! Come here! Chester!"

Russ waited patiently for Rusty to stop shouting, but the kid was determined to find Chester—whoever that was. Finally, Russ couldn't stand it any longer and snapped, "Hey, kid! Stop that yelling! Who's Chester?"

"My dog," Rusty answered. "The dog I'm going to get when I grow up." He walked over to where Russ was sitting. "You know, Chester, the world's greatest dog, who rides in the back of my truck and plays Frisbee and goes everywhere I go." He started whistling. "Chester! Here, boy! Come on, boy!"

Russ watched him for a moment with a look of pity on his face. "Hey, kid," he said. "Harsh news. There's no dog here."

Rusty looked crushed. "What do you mean?" he asked.

"There's no dog here. I don't own a dog," Russ answered.

"No dog?" cried the kid. "I grow up to be a guy with no dog? Why?"

"Because I don't want a dog," Russ said with a shrug. "I couldn't take care of one. I travel all the time for work."

Ooh! That sounded exciting. Rusty liked this news. "I travel for work?" he asked. "I grow up to fly jets, right? I knew it!"

"No . . ." said Russ, looking uncomfortable.

"No?" asked Rusty. "Well, what do I do?"

Russ hesitated for a second. "You're a consultant," he answered. "An image consultant."

"What's that?" asked Rusty. "What do I *do*?"

"You don't *do* anything," said Russ. "You tell other people what to do. You boss everybody around, and they do what you tell them."

The kid stared at him. The more he found out about his future, the more worried he became. He looked around Russ's house. Besides Chester, something else seemed to be missing. "Shouldn't there be a lady here?" asked Rusty.

"You mean living here?" replied Russ. "No. I live alone."

"I thought you said you were forty!" shouted Rusty.

"I am," said Russ.

The kid's face got all squished up. "Let me get this straight: I'm forty, I'm not married, I don't fly jets, and I don't have a dog?" He paused. Then he wailed, "I grow up to be a loser!"

Russ just stared at him, shocked.


That night, as Russ tossed and turned in his bed, Rusty sat out on the deck, singing loudly to himself. "John Jacob Jingle-Heimer-Smith. That's my name, too! Whenever I go out, the people always shout, there goes John Jacob Jingle-Heimer-Smith! NANANANANANA!"

Russ pressed his face into his pillow and tried to block out the noise. Suddenly, he heard the kid scream, "AHHHH!"

Russ jumped out of bed, lunged to the window, and looked out at Rusty jumping around on the deck below him. "Wow! Look at that!" Rusty said, pointing up at the moon.

Russ mocked him, *"Wow! Look at it! It's the moon! It's up in the sky! It does that!* You travel thirty years across time and *this* is what you're screaming about?"

"I'm sorry," said the kid. "I'll never get excited again. *Obviously.*"

Russ got ready to shut the window. Rusty asked, "Can I please come in now? I'm cold."

Russ replied, "It's seventy degrees out. You're not cold."

"Wait," called the kid. "Just let me ask you a question. Why does the moon look orange sometimes?"

"Because it . . . because there's . . ." Russ started to answer, before he realized that he didn't know. "Go away!" he yelled and slammed the window shut.

Rusty yelled up at him, "I knew it! I grow up to be a guy who doesn't know anything! And who doesn't have a dog!"

# Chapter 7

The next morning, Russ and Amy were sitting with three men at a window table in a fancy restaurant. Russ was looking like his old self again. When he had woken up that morning, Rusty was gone! Not on the deck. Not in the house. Nowhere. Maybe he had really disappeared!

Now Russ could finally focus on work again. The client they were meeting with this morning dressed like a hippie, with long, tangled hair and a long, bushy beard. Russ was trying to tell him that he needed to change his image for the public.

"Let me give it to you straight, Vivian," Russ started. "If you want to make the *Fortune* 500, you have to realize that people are going to want to take a look at you."

All of a sudden, Russ's attention was drawn to someone outside the window. Oh, no. It was Rusty.

Though he tried to ignore the kid, Russ looked shaken and started to stammer. Amy noticed the kid and turned to Russ, asking, "Someone you know?"

"Huh?" said Russ, distracted. "No. Of course not."

Just then, Rusty waved right at Russ and called out, "Russ! Russ Duritz!"

Now Russ couldn't deny knowing the kid. He jumped up from the table, excusing himself. Then he ran out of the restaurant and pulled Rusty aside.

"I thought you had disappeared!" Russ said to him.

Rusty held up his hands. "I don't know how to disappear," he said. "And I'm hungry!"

Just then, Amy came up to join them. She held out her hand to Rusty. "Hi, I'm Amy. Who are you?"

"I'm Rusty," answered the kid.

Amy gave Russ a "Who is this?" look. Russ thought fast. "My nephew," he burst out.

Amy raised her eyebrows. "Your nephew?" she asked, not buying it. "The kid who's going to college in the fall?"

"No, the youngest one," Russ said, scrambling for an explanation. "The one my sister never talks about."

Amy had known Russ long enough to know that something funny was going on. She turned to Rusty. "Are you having fun with your 'uncle'?"

"Not really," Rusty answered. "He made me sleep outside. He didn't give me any breakfast. And he doesn't have a dog."

"That *is* a problem," said Amy, shooting Russ a look. "How about we go inside and have some bacon and eggs?"

"He doesn't have time," Russ insisted. "We're leaving right now."

"What about our client?" Amy asked.

"Handle it for me," Russ told her as he dragged Rusty away.

Dr. Alexander was in the middle of a session with a nervous patient, Mr. Mott, who was holding a large white cat on his lap, when Russ came bursting into her office.

"I'm in the middle of a session," Dr. Alexander said to Russ with a stern look. "Your appointment is at four o'clock."

"But those pills you gave me aren't working," Russ exclaimed.

Dr. Alexander asked Russ once more to leave her office. But Mr. Mott interrupted. "Wait a minute, Doctor. He seems really distressed." Then to Russ he said, "Do you suffer from delusions? I do. What do *you* see?"

"A boy . . ." said Russ, ". . . who's really me."

Mr. Mott was impressed. "That's very original," he said.

"He's here. Right now," said Russ. "Don't you want to see him?"

"I do," said Mr. Mott. He set down his cat and went to the office door. He opened it and peered out into the waiting room. When he turned back, he said to Dr. Alexander, "This man's inner child is out in the lobby reading *National Geographic*!"

Russ called Rusty into the room. "Hi," he said shyly to Dr. Alexander.

"Does this look like a hallucination to you?" Russ asked the doctor.

"No. This is not a hallucination," she answered. "This is a real child. A child who looks something like you. But this is not you."

"Let's show her," Russ told the kid.

Together, they showed the doctor their identical physical traits. They pulled up their pant legs to show their scars. They pulled down their collars to show their moles. And they cracked their knuckles at the same time.

"I swear, this kid is me, Doctor," Russ argued. "When I was eight, I was a fat, lisping, dorky-looking, flood-wearing, pathetic little crybaby spaz exactly like this!"

Dr. Alexander did not look impressed. "I see how important this is to you, Mr. Duritz. But you need to come back at four. Then I will help you. All right?"

"The question is," Mr. Mott offered, "why is he here? There's got to be a reason." Mr. Mott scratched his head, thinking. Then an idea seemed to come to him. "You know everything because you've already lived it. Which means you know something he needs to know. Or something he's got to do. Got it?"

"No," said the other three together. Even Dr. Alexander looked confused.

"What?" said Mr. Mott to his cat. He knelt in front of the animal, listening. Finally, he stood up and said to them, "Give him what he came for, then he'll go away. Give him what he came for, all will be put right."

Shaking their heads, Russ and Rusty left the doctor's office and made their way outside.

As they started off down the street, the shadow of a small plane passed over them. But they were both too busy talking to notice.

"Maybe the cat is right," said Rusty.

"Oh, yeah," said Russ. "Of course the cat is

right. *Why wouldn't he be?* I don't know what's worse: that I'm stuck with you, or that I have no idea what to do about it!" Russ plopped down onto the curb, at a total loss.

"Why don't we get something to eat?" suggested Rusty.

"Why?" Russ asked. "Because you don't know what to do, so you want to stuff your face?"

"No," the kid answered, "Because it says to, up there in the sky."

Russ followed Rusty's pointing finger and saw skywriting. A small plane was just flying away after writing the last of the big white letters that spelled out EAT HERE. Russ looked down from the writing to see the Skyway Diner right across the street. It was the same diner that Russ had chased the kid into that night at the airport.

Russ and Rusty walked into the coffee shop. The kid ordered a huge meal, and Russ ordered coffee.

"'Give him what he came for,'" Russ said, repeating Mr. Mott's words. "Okay, I'm asking. What *did* you come for?"

"I dunno," answered Rusty. "The model airplane?"

"You already got that," Russ pointed out, shaking his head. "What am I going to do with you?"

"What do you want to do with me?" asked Rusty.

Russ looked out the window of the coffee shop and pondered the question. "What do I want to do?" Russ asked. "Put you on a diet. Get you into track. Why wait until you're twenty? Cut your hair, maybe dye it blond with a blue streak. Get you some decent clothes. Get this commercial director I know to put you in something hip so that the girls will like you. Put you with a skateboard pro I know who could . . . Of course! This is what you came for! Why didn't I see this before? I need to give *you* an image update. This is what I do for a living!"

The kid looked uncertain.

"Making people look good is what I do. If I can do it for movie stars and politicians," Russ continued, "I can do it for myself. Now, the only question is, with so much to do, where should we start?"

"Well," said Rusty, "I'd like not to get my butt kicked so much. You know someone who can teach me how to fight?"

Russ smiled. "Oh, I think I can scrounge someone up."

# Chapter 8

**A** pool party was in full swing at a big Bel Air mansion. Russ and Rusty headed straight for the cabana, where Kenny Gordon, Russ's client, was trying on tuxedo jackets. Kenny was a big, powerfully built boxer. His fiancée, Giselle, and Amy were looking on, helping Kenny decide what to wear at his wedding the next day.

A pizza delivery man arrived and set down a large pizza. When Rusty reached for a piece, Russ stopped him, saying, "No way!"

Kenny, a little overweight, smiled at the kid. "He won't let you eat either, huh? Who are you, anyway?"

Amy answered, "This is Russ's nephew, Rusty."

Rusty spotted Kenny's dogs, two huge St. Bernards, playing on the lawn. "I love your dogs," he said to Kenny. "I wish *I* had one."

"Well," said Kenny, "someday when you grow up, you will."

"No, I won't," announced Rusty, shooting Russ a look.

Russ interrupted. "Hey, Kenny, I want to use your ring to give Pudge-Boy here a boxing lesson. Maybe you could step in and show him a few moves?"

"Be happy to," answered Kenny. "That way, he can knock your lights out the next time you call him 'Pudge-Boy.'"

In the boxing ring, Kenny and Rusty faced each other. Russ, Amy, Giselle, and the other guests gathered around to watch the lesson. Next to Kenny, the kid looked tiny. He only came up to Kenny's bellybutton.

Kenny started the lesson. "You've got to move, dance around," he said, demonstrating some fancy footwork. "Use the balls of your feet, learn to weave. Forward, back, left, right. Your feet move you away from the punches."

Rusty tried moving around. Russ rolled his eyes, thinking to himself that the kid looked incredibly lame. But Giselle was encouraging. "That's right. You're getting it!" she said.

"Now," Kenny said, "think about your hands. You've got to block the punch, right?"

Rusty put his hands up in front of his face and instinctively blocked as Kenny jabbed his glove. Then Kenny surprised Rusty by jabbing him lightly in the belly. Just a tap, but the kid was already overwhelmed.

"You see?" Kenny asked. "It's going to be coming from all directions—just like life. Now, let's put you together with someone more your own size." He took off his gloves and tossed them over to Russ.

The bell rang—*clang!*—and Russ and Rusty started dancing around each other in the ring. But Russ was not going to be as gentle as Kenny was. He swiped Rusty a few times. The kid tried to fight back, but it was no use. Watching from ringside, Amy grew concerned and tried to distract Russ. "Hey, Russ! You're so ugly, you're *forty!*"

Russ couldn't help himself. He stopped to scowl at Amy. When he did, Rusty punched him in the stomach—a solid one—and Russ fell to his knees. The kid jumped on Russ and pushed him to the ground.

"Hey! Cut it out!" Russ cried. But Rusty wasn't listening. He kept on whaling Russ, taking out all of his frustrations on him.

Kenny rushed into the ring and spoke into Rusty's ear. "Hey, little tiger. We don't hit 'em when they're down."

"Yeah?" said the kid. "They hit *me* when I'm down!"

"Who?" asked Kenny.

"The kids at school," answered Rusty.

A different look came over Kenny's face. "Why didn't you say so?" he said. "That's street fighting, not boxing. Show him the head scissors, Russ."

With that, Russ wrapped his legs around the kid's neck and peeled him off his chest, headfirst. Rusty landed with a *thump* on his back.

He lay there with a big grin on his face. "Hey!" he said. "Now *that's* a move I can use!"

Russ and Rusty laughed identical laughs. Then, at the same time, they both scratched an itch and tucked their arms behind their heads in the exact same way. Amy was watching them . . . and becoming very suspicious.

Amy turned to Giselle. "Have you noticed how alike those two are?" she asked Giselle.

Giselle just shrugged. "Makes sense. They're related, right?"

"Hmmm . . ." Amy said to herself.

# Chapter 9

**S**tanding in Kenny's driveway, Russ got out his cell phone and called his office to check messages.

Janet picked up. "Oh, hello!" she said. "When I hadn't heard from you in four hours, I assumed you were dead. I called your life insurance company, but they said I'm not your beneficiary. What's up with that? By the way, how's 'Mini-You?'"

Just then, Russ spotted Amy helping Rusty into her car.

"Hey!" Russ shouted to Amy. "Where are you going?"

"We're going to my place for dessert," Amy shouted back. "Meet us there!"

At Amy's house, the kid was wandering around, looking at her stuff. Amy watched him, growing more and more suspicious. When he came over to her, Amy reached out and lifted the hair off Rusty's neck. She found just what she was afraid she'd find: the same mole that was on Russ's neck, and in the exact same place.

Minutes later, Russ came through Amy's front door. Amy yanked him aside. She was furious. "He's your son!" she hissed at Russ. "He's your son, you have a son, and all this time you never breathed a word! And you're some deadbeat dad who had visitation rights today or something and . . . who's the mom, anyway?"

Rusty overheard what was going on and came over. "I'm not his son," he said. "Honest."

"Then who are you?" Amy asked.

Rusty looked at Russ. "We have to tell her," he said.

Russ just shook his head no.

"Tell me what?" Amy asked, looking from one to the other.

Rusty pulled down his collar to show his mole. But Russ wasn't going along. Back and forth, Russ and the kid argued about whether to tell Amy that they were the same person. As they argued, Amy backed away from them and went to her desk. She rummaged through some drawers and finally found what she was looking for: a photograph. It pictured a smiling young mother with her arm wrapped around a geeky-looking kid. But not just any kid. It was Russ, at the same age as Rusty. Amy couldn't believe her eyes. She looked back and forth between Rusty and the photo. Even their shirts were the same! Russ and the kid stopped arguing as they realized what was happening. Amy was convinced. She sank to the floor in shock, dropping the photograph.

Later, Amy and Russ sat on the sofa talking while Rusty watched television. The kid was completely unaware of the adults. He lolled on the floor, pulling up his T-shirt and scratching his soft, tubby belly. Then he started picking his nose. Russ was humiliated by his 8-year-old self. "I'm so embarrassing," he groaned to Amy.

Amy replied, "You don't get it . . . you're not embarrassing. You're adorable."

"Which explains why you have that picture of me in your drawer?" he said sarcastically.

Amy replied defensively. "I have that picture because you asked me to make you copies! When that journalist profiled you, remember?"

Russ dropped the issue and they looked back at Rusty, who was now licking his ice cream bowl and getting ice cream all over his face. Amy was mesmerized.

"You don't hate me for being like that?" Russ asked, pointing to the kid.

"No, of course not!" Amy said. "Why?"

"Amy," said Russ, "when I am him, I go to the desert with my family one summer. I find the only mud puddle in the Mojave and fall in it. When I am him, I am a ring bearer in a wedding. I trip over my own feet on the way up the aisle. They *still* haven't found the rings. When I look at him, all I see is a lot of horrible memories."

Amy reached out and touched Russ's cheek, wanting to comfort him.

Suddenly, Russ's cell phone rang. It was Kenny. His ring bearer had gotten sick and he wanted to know if Rusty could fill in. Russ winced.

# Chapter 10

**R**usty walked up the church aisle at Kenny and Giselle's wedding, wearing a tuxedo and concentrating very hard.

As the kid passed the row where Amy and Russ were sitting, Russ caught his eye and clearly mouthed the words, "Don't trip!"

Just then, Rusty tripped over his own feet and fell on his face, right in the middle of the aisle. The church was silent as everyone listened to the sound of rings rolling away.

Russ smacked his forehead and said, "Moron!"

Several wedding guests whirled around to glare at Russ. A guest standing right behind him muttered, "Jerk."

At the wedding reception, Rusty helped himself to several pieces of the wedding cake while Russ danced with the mother of the groom. Amy was over with the wedding party, taking pictures. As he ate, Rusty watched Russ and Amy. Amy was talking and laughing, and looked so beautiful. Rusty looked at the newlyweds . . . then at Russ . . . and Amy . . . and back again. Suddenly, his mouth dropped open as an amazing idea came to him.

He rushed out onto the dance floor, where Russ was dancing. The kid pulled on Russ's jacket to get his attention. "I figured it out!" he cried.

"You're interrupting," Russ hissed.

"But I figured it out! What I came for! And I have to tell you right *now*!" Rusty cried desperately.

"Now is not a good time," Russ said, shooing him away.

Giving up on Russ, Rusty threw up his hands and stomped off to find Amy, who was putting more film in her camera. Rusty grabbed a rose from a nearby centerpiece and dropped it into Amy's lap. He said, "Amy? I have a question. A big one."

From the dance floor, Russ looked over at the kid with Amy and noticed how lovely Amy looked. Suddenly he felt very drawn to her. But a second later, he had pushed the thought away and continued dancing.

On the other side of the room, Rusty was getting down on one knee in front of Amy. "I know we haven't known each other very long," Rusty said to her, "but in case I never get around to asking you . . ."

Just then, Russ glanced over again and saw the kid in the standard marriage proposal stance. What was Rusty doing? He knew this could only mean trouble. He left his dance partner and rushed over just as Rusty asked, "Will you marry me?"

As Amy sat there, in shock, Russ picked up the kid and rushed out into the hallway. Amy ran after them.

"He asked me a question," she called to Russ once they were in the hall. "Don't you want to hear what I was going to say?"

"No!" said Russ, looking flustered.

"Yes!" said Rusty.

"I was going to say . . . that I have to think about it," continued Amy.

"Oh, really," Russ said. "You have to think about it?"

"Yes," answered Amy. "Because *impossibly*, what would previously have seemed to me to be the worst idea in the universe has, over the last twelve hours, come to seem like a not-so-terrible idea, opening up a very small window of opportunity for you . . ."

"And what if I don't want to take that opportunity?" Russ asked her.

"Well, a part of you obviously does," Amy snapped. "And it is that part of you that is causing me to think about it!"

"Then think about it!" Russ burst out.

Both Russ and Amy were shocked by what had just happened. Russ stammered and rushed off to find the valet and get his car. Amy watched him go, stunned. Suddenly, she heard Rusty laughing. She turned to see him watching the television in the hotel bar. She looked up to see what was so funny . . . and she couldn't believe her eyes. Right there, playing on the television, was the videotape she had shot of Bob Riley getting pied by the kids— the tape that Russ had supposedly thrown in the trash.

At that moment, Russ came back in. He took one look at Amy's face and knew that something was wrong.

Amy couldn't believe Russ would do this. "You crawled through that Dumpster after I left?" she asked Russ.

"No, I didn't crawl through . . ." Russ started to answer.

"Of course not," Amy interrupted. "You sent Janet to do it!" She was absolutely furious.

Russ was silent. He didn't know what to say. Then suddenly, he struck back. "Poor Amy. Mixed up with a rotten guy who feels obligated to his clients. Must be tough. You know what the number-one killer of women photographers under forty is?"

"Russ," said Amy, interrupting his standard line, "I am not pitying myself here. I am pitying *you*." Amy leaned down and gave Rusty a big hug. "I'm so sorry," she told him. Then she looked at Russ. "The saddest part of this whole thing," she said, motioning to the kid, "is that you *could* have been great!" She whirled around and walked off, leaving Russ and Rusty behind.

# Chapter 11

**B**ack home, in Russ's bedroom, Rusty was very upset about what had happened with Amy. Russ had tried to cheer him up, but the kid wouldn't even crack a smile. For a good while, Russ and Rusty ·did not speak. Then, finally, as Rusty got into bed on Russ's sofa that night, he said, "You know, it's our birthday tomorrow."

"Yeah, I know," said Russ.

"What happens next?" Rusty asked excitedly. "I mean, to me. Between being me and becoming you. What happens?"

Russ really wasn't in the mood to go through his whole life story. But Rusty looked so hopeful. Russ sighed. "Okay," he said. "You make it through grade school alive. Barely. But in high school, while you continue to be ugly, you are no longer stupid. You work your butt off, and you get good grades. Very good. And you end up winning a full scholarship to UCLA. College is a lot better than grade school. You make the track team, find a speech therapist for your lisp, work your butt off and graduate at the top of your class. You end up going for a master's in business school . . . where you also work your butt off. Story of your life."

"Sounds like a lot to look forward to," Rusty said sarcastically.

"Well, the good news is that while you are currently a pathetic dweeb, eventually you become *this* rich, high-powered chick magnet," said Russ, striking a pose.

"Who doesn't have a dog. Or a chick," Rusty reminded him.

"Is that all you see when you look at me?" asked Russ. "A dogless, chickless guy?"

"With a twitch," the kid answered.

"Nice," said Russ.

"When do I get that?" asked Rusty.

"I don't remember," said Russ.

As Russ turned out the light and headed for the door, Rusty said, "I get what you do now. I mean, I get what I do when I grow up. For a living. You help people lie about who they really are so they can pretend they're somebody else. Right?"

Russ had never heard it put that way before.

Was that really what his job amounted to? "That's pretty good," Russ said at last. He said good night to Rusty and he closed the door quietly behind him.

In the living room, Russ switched on the television to watch the local news. Well, what do you know? The news anchorwoman, looking out at him from the TV screen, was the same woman he had sat next to on the airplane. Russ was pleased to see that Deirdre had transformed herself exactly according to his directions: she had cut her hair, toned down her makeup, and bought better jewelry. As Russ watched, Deirdre began the newscast with a cheerful "Good evening, *y'all*." He smiled in spite of himself.

Later that evening, as Deirdre left the television station, a voice called out to her. "I heard the 'y'all.' It's a showstopper."

Deirdre turned her head to see Russ leaning against a wall next to the door. "Why, it's the image consultant," she said with a smile. Then for a second she looked worried and put a hand to her head. "Don't tell me . . . my hair's still too big."

"No, you were perfect," Russ said. "Can I buy you a cup of coffee?"

They found a nearby restaurant and sat down to talk. There was something about Deirdre that made Russ feel he could tell her the whole weird story: about the planes, the kid, Amy. When he was done, Deirdre just sat back and said, "That is the strangest story I have ever heard in my life." She shrugged. "But it makes perfect sense to me."

"It does?" Russ said.

"Sure," she said. "Why wouldn't your eight-year-old self time-travel out here to give you a hand? You're obviously in trouble and he wants to straighten you out."

"*He* wants to straighten *me* out?" Russ asked.

"Of course," Deirdre said with a chuckle. "You didn't think it was the other way around, did you?" From the look on Russ's face, she could tell that he was guilty as charged. "Look, darlin', you're turning forty tomorrow and you haven't acquired a single thing of any real value in your life. Money doesn't count. You're virtually friendless, you barely talk to your family, and you just lost the only woman in the world who's ever meant anything to you."

"Oh my god!" was all that Russ could say as he realized that Deirdre was absolutely right.

Russ was still digesting what Deirdre had said as the two of them walked through the parking lot on their way home. "All this time I've been thinking he's here so I can improve him. Teach him things," Russ said.

"Well, maybe he's here for you to teach him things . . . or maybe he's here for you to remember things. Ever think of that?" Deirdre asked.

"Not until now," said Russ. He looked at Deirdre. He couldn't say good night without asking one question. "That day we met on the plane, you said I was talking in my sleep . . ."

Deirdre smiled. "I thought you'd never ask," she said. "You were saying 'help me' over and over again. Do you remember who you were saying it to?"

The details of the dream came flooding back to Russ. Yes, he remembered all right. He had been shouting to the pilot in the propeller plane. But he didn't know why. Russ looked up at Deirdre, not ready to share these thoughts with her. He shook his head no.

"Well," she said, "don't stop asking for help, Russ. You just might get it." And with a "Bye, y'all" and a wiggle of her red fingernails, she was gone.

# Chapter 12

**A**fter midnight that night, Russ walked through the front door of his house, quietly talking to Janet on his cell phone. "I'm not coming in tomorrow," he said. "You'll have to cancel everything and move it to Friday."

"Okay," said Janet. "Anything else?"

"Yes," Russ told her. "Find out why the full moon looks orange sometimes when it rises." Then he hung up the phone and looked through the house, trying to find the kid. He found him in his bedroom, where Rusty was fast asleep in his bed. Russ walked over to him and gently shook him awake. "Happy birthday!"

Rusty opened his eyes and smiled. "To us," he said.

"I'm ready now," Russ announced to him, "to find out what you came for. Want to help?"

It was three in the morning. Russ and Rusty sat down at the kitchen table—Russ with a cup of coffee, the kid with a glass of milk—and talked about their childhood.

"*Anything* about me?" Rusty asked.

"Anything that will take me back," Russ answered.

"You mean like . . . I like to help Dad when he works on the car, but if I do something wrong, he yells at me. Sometimes he buys me ice cream afterward. But still I don't like to mess up. Like last week, I lost a screw and I was afraid to tell him. I found it later in my pocket. Look, I still have it." Rusty reached into his pocket, pulled out the screw, and showed it to Russ.

As the sun came up, Russ and Rusty went for a walk on the beach, still talking.

The kid was saying, "I like to go to the store with Mom. She lets me read the comic books while she shops. She makes chocolate-chip pancakes every Sunday morning. At least, she used to before she started getting tired all the time."

"Tired all the time?" Russ asked, with a puzzled look on his face. "Is that what you think?"

"Well," Rusty answered, "she stays in bed a lot. You don't remember that?"

Russ felt a twinge of pain, but he tried to keep it

from showing on his face. "Yeah, I remember," he said. "Keep going."

As they hopped into Russ's convertible and drove around, Rusty told Russ all about his best friend, Tim Wheaton. Well, he was Rusty's best friend until Tim started to hang around with Vince and his tough crowd of boys. Tim threw a rock at Rusty and they hadn't been friends since.

"He threw a rock at us?" asked Russ with a defensive look. "What happened?"

"Oh, those guys get together every recess in the corner of the playground, where they like to pick on kids," Rusty explained.

"Behind the kindergarten? Where there's that really big slide?" asked Russ.

"Yeah!" shouted the kid. "You're remembering!"

He *was* remembering. "Keep going. Don't stop," said Russ, as their car entered a long, dark tunnel.

"There's like five of them," continued Rusty. And they're really mean. And the worst thing about them is they're mean to cats and dogs. Especially this one three-legged dog . . ."

"Tripod!" Russ cried. "I know this!" Russ stopped and thought for a second, remembering . . . putting two and two together. Then as he looked over at Rusty, his face cleared. "I know now what happens! I know why you're here.

I know everything! It was my birthday . . . my eighth birthday . . . it was thirty-two years ago today!"

At that moment, as they came driving out of the tunnel into the sunshine, they heard the roar of a small propeller plane as it flew out of the tunnel just behind them. Where in the world did it come from?

And what had happened to their car? Russ and Rusty looked down and saw that they were no longer driving a 2000 Porsche. Instead, they were riding in a 1960s model. Even Russ's clothes had changed! Now he was wearing a late '60s outfit. Could this mean what they thought it meant? Had they really just time-traveled backward?

"We did it!" Russ cried.

"Am I home?" Rusty asked. "Is it really nineteen sixty-eight?"

A VW bus drove by with daisy decals stuck to it. "No question about it," Russ announced, laughing. "What time is it?"

"Ten-fifteen," Rusty told him.

"We've got to hurry," Russ said. "Recess is at ten-thirty. We change our lives in just fifteen minutes!"

Russ and Rusty stood on the playground as dozens of kids ran screaming out of the school. Russ did not have much time to tell the kid what was about to happen.

"Okay, here's what I remember," said Russ. "Your eighth birthday is one of the worst days of your life. There's a fistfight, and you get creamed."

Rusty scoffed. "So? That happens all the time."

"Yeah, but this time it's worse," Russ continued. "Some boys try to torture Tripod, and you get seriously thrashed. You go down after only one punch. You solidify your status as a victim for the next eight years . . . all the way through high school."

"Oh, boy," said Rusty, looking scared. He was not looking forward to this.

Russ continued: "Vince Kajinski and his friends are going to say something to get you back behind the building. But when you go around the corner with them, they're going to have Tripod tied up. That's where you're going to fight."

Just then, Vince Kajinski and his gang came around the corner of the school. Rusty looked nervous. Russ didn't feel so good himself.

Russ put a hand on the kid's shoulder. "We could stop this here, you know," he said. "You don't have to go with them. You could go hang out with a teacher. Stay inside through recess."

Rusty thought it over, but said, "No. If I don't go with them today, I'll have to fight them tomorrow, or the next day. And today, *you're* here with me."

"That's right," Russ assured him. "Today I'm here."

"I can do this," Rusty told himself. "Get in close, uppercut, *pow, pow*." With that, he walked away from Russ, to the middle of the playground, where he looked lost and alone.

As if on cue, Vince called out to him, "Hey, Rusty! Come over here."

Mark, one of Vince's buddies, said, "It's your birthday, right? We've got a birthday present for you."

The kid took one last look at Russ and walked toward the boys and around the corner of the building. Just as Russ had said, he found two other kids there guarding Tripod, the three-legged dog. The poor animal had a rope around his neck and a string of firecrackers attached to his tail. He was terrified and kept trying to escape, but the boys held him back with sticks.

Rusty told the boys to let Tripod go.

Mark answered, "That stinkin' three-legged dog is worthless. We want to see him run. Light the firecrackers and we'll give you one of these leather bracelets. Then you can be one of us." Mark held out his wrist to show off his bracelet.

Rusty surprised them with an insult. "You guys are dirtbags. I don't want to hang out with you. Let the dog go."

Vince couldn't believe that Rusty was standing

up to them. He lunged forward and smacked Rusty on the chin. Rusty fell down, but then popped right back up again. He was ready for whatever the boys had in store for him. The other boys formed a circle around Rusty and Vince, watching the fight.

Vince hit Rusty again, and Rusty doubled over, gasping for air. Watching from a distance, Russ could barely contain himself. He wanted to run and help the kid. But then Rusty stood up and set his feet, just as Kenny had shown him. Now Rusty could easily step out of the way of Vince's blows. Rusty reached out and popped Vince on the chin. Vince wasn't hurt, but he looked stunned that Rusty had landed a punch.

Now more determined than ever, Vince started to fight dirty. He stepped forward as if to throw a punch, but instead he whipped his leg around and kicked Rusty in the side of the knee. Rusty yelled in pain and dropped to the ground. Vince jumped on him immediately, throwing punches. But Rusty remembered the head scissors move. He wrapped his legs around Vince's neck and flipped the bigger kid off of him.

Both boys got to their feet, and Vince came at Rusty one last time, throwing punches. Rusty avoided the first of them, and landed a punch right on Vince's nose. But then Vince landed a wallop, and Rusty fell to his knees. Vince pounced and kept on punching him. It looked like the fight was over. Russ couldn't bear it any longer. He started to come over to break up the fight. But Rusty saw him coming and shook his head.

Then, all of a sudden, Rusty threw out his leg, tripping Vince. When Vince fell, Rusty climbed on top of him and started throwing punches. Vince was defeated! "Say uncle! Say uncle!" Rusty demanded. As soon as Vince said it, Rusty climbed off him, breathing heavily.

The other boys looked at Rusty with newfound respect. As the class bell rang, Mark walked up to Rusty and said, "Don't let the teachers see you like this. They'll make you stay after school." Then all the boys, including Vince, ran off. The kid rushed to Tripod and untied him, taking the firecrackers off his tail. Tripod licked the dirt from Rusty's face.

Russ ran up to Rusty. "You did it!"

"Yahoo!" Rusty answered. "I did what I had to do. So that's it, right?"

Russ looked up to see the principal and one of the teachers walking toward Rusty, and suddenly the memories of that day came back to him in a flood of emotion. "No, kid," he said. "I'm afraid it's about to get worse. Much worse."

# Chapter 13

The kid sat alone in the principal's office, wiping some blood from his nose with a handkerchief. Russ waited outside in the hallway. He watched as two people walked past him, opened the door, and entered the principal's office.

Rusty looked up to see the principal enter, along with his mom. She looked very sick; drawn and frail. As soon as she walked in, Rusty yelled, "Mom!" and ran to hug her. "I'm sorry, Mom, I'm sorry," he sobbed.

"Shhh," she said. "It's okay. It's okay, now." Mrs. Duritz stroked Rusty's hot, messy face.

Then the principal spoke. "I'm sorry you had to come in, Mrs. Duritz. We all know you haven't been well."

"Please don't punish him, Principal Graham," Mrs. Duritz said. "Today is his birthday."

• • •

Mrs. Duritz and Rusty climbed out of their car in the driveway of their house. Russ pulled up on the street behind them. Struggling to look normal, Mrs. Duritz made her way, slowly, up the front walk. Rusty followed a few steps behind.

Just then, Mr. Duritz pulled up in his car, home from work. When he saw his wife, he jumped out of the car and cried, "Gloria! Are you out of your mind? What are you doing up?"

Mrs. Duritz took another step or two, then collapsed against her husband. He lifted her up into his arms and rushed into the house. Rusty followed them up the porch steps. But before he could enter the house, his father turned and barked, "Stay there!"

Russ looked on from across the street, his cheek twitching.

The kid waited outside—alone. After a minute or two, Mr. Duritz came back out of the house, his face red with rage. "What's the matter with you?" he asked his son.

"I'm sorry," Rusty said. "I'm sorry."

"How could you do this to your mother?" his father yelled. "What are you trying to do? Kill her faster?"

Rusty was shocked by his father's words. "What?"

"She's dying," his father said. "We're going to lose her. And you pull a stunt like you did today?" As Rusty's eyes filled with tears, his father shook him furiously. "You've got to learn to take care of yourself. Do you understand'?"

Rusty blinked back his tears. "I found the screw, Dad," he announced. He tried not to cry as he pulled the screw from his pocket. The tears overwhelmed him as he offered it to his father.

But Mr. Duritz knocked the screw from his hand. "Stop crying!" he told his son.

"I'm not crying," Rusty insisted.

"I said *stop*!" Mr. Duritz shouted as he pressed his fingers against Rusty's eyelids. He was trying desperately to stop Rusty's tears. At that moment, Rusty's cheek twitched. It was Russ's twitch. And it was happening to Rusty for the first time at that moment.

"Grow up!" Mr. Duritz shouted at Rusty again, and then he turned and rushed into the house.

The kid walked slowly back down the porch stairs and across the street to where Russ was standing.

"Mom's dying," he told Russ.

"I know," Russ answered.

"Soon?" Rusty asked.

"Before your next birthday," Russ told him

gently, pulling the kid to his chest. "You didn't do it. She has cancer. The cancer's doing it. Dad was just saying that because he's scared. He knows he's going to have to raise you alone, and he doesn't know how."

Russ was crying now, too. Rusty felt Russ's tears land on him. He brushed at them.

"I thought you never cried," the kid said to him.

"Not since my eighth birthday," Russ answered. "Apparently, I'm starting up again."

"Somebody call the *whaambulance*," Rusty said. Russ and the kid laughed, hugging each other.

Finally Russ said, "Come on, let's get out of here. Let's get something to eat."

# Chapter 14

Russ and Rusty found the Skyway Diner. It was after dark, and the two talked about the day's events and how they would affect their lives.

"What's done is done," Russ announced. "It's our birthday. Let's celebrate."

They sang "Happy Birthday" to each other and reminisced about other childhood memories. Then Russ looked seriously at Rusty and said, "I won't let you down anymore."

"Promise?" Rusty asked.

"Promise," Russ answered.

Just then, a golden retriever trotted by their table and stuck his nose in Rusty's lap. The kid embraced the dog and started to pet him.

From the other end of the coffee shop, a man called, "Chester! Come over here!"

Russ and Rusty froze and looked at each other as

the dog squirmed away and ran toward the voice.

"Did you hear what he just called his dog?" Rusty asked Russ.

*"Chester?"* Russ said in amazement.

At the same moment, Russ and Rusty turned to look at the dog's owner. He was a pilot, about 70 years old, but his face was turned away from them. They couldn't see what he looked like.

Then as Russ and Rusty watched, a car pulled up in front of the restaurant. When the pilot looked out the window and saw it, he whistled for Chester and went outside to meet it. Russ and Rusty rose from the table, their eyes wide, while Russ threw money down to pay their bill. He and the kid followed the pilot outside.

The car pulled up to a small airplane waiting on the runway, and the pilot—still facing away from Russ and Rusty—opened the door to help his wife, son, daughter-in-law, and grandchild out of the car and into the plane. Russ and Rusty stood and watched from a distance. But even from there, they both noticed that his wife looked a lot like Amy.

When the rest of the family was loaded into the plane, the pilot finally turned to face Russ and the kid. And it was him. It was Russ Duritz at age 70. Russ and Rusty just stood there with their mouths open, unable to speak.

The pilot just smiled at them and motioned to the plane. "Do you like it?" he asked them.

Russ and Rusty nodded.

Finally, Russ got a few words out. "How did you . . . I mean . . . *why*?"

"You asked me to come, remember?" the pilot answered. "In your dreams. You called for help."

"So *everything*? Even the model airplane . . . ?" Russ asked.

The pilot nodded. "That was just my way of breaking the ice!"

Russ, Rusty, and the pilot were silent for a moment, staring at each other and thinking about their present, their past, and their future.

"Well, the family's waiting," the pilot finally said. "I'll bet you've got a lot of questions."

"Yes, I do," Russ replied.

"I wouldn't worry about it," the pilot said. "You've got thirty years to figure out the answers." Then he smiled at Rusty and said, "It was especially nice to see you again."

"See ya," said Rusty.

The pilot climbed into his plane and waved good–bye. As Russ and Rusty watched, it taxied down the runway and took off toward a huge orange moon hanging low in the sky.

When it lifted off the ground, Russ and Rusty

burst out screaming and laughing for joy. "We did it! We did it!" They danced around the tarmac, celebrating.

"Did you see our dog?" asked the kid breathlessly. "Did you see our family? And we fly! I'm a pilot!"

Russ lifted his arms to the sky and cried, "I . . . am . . . not . . . a . . . *loser*!"

They watched the plane grow smaller and smaller in the sky. After a moment, Russ said, "Can you believe it, kid?" He took his eyes from the sky and looked down. "Kid?" He couldn't believe it. Rusty was gone. He turned around. The coffee shop was gone, too. Suddenly, Russ found himself standing alone on the runway, back in the present, wearing his present-day clothes again.

He could hardly breathe. Had he dreamed it all? Russ didn't know. But the kid was gone, and Russ was on his own again. Finally, he knew exactly what he had to do.

# Chapter 15

**B**right and early the next morning, Janet rushed into Russ's house, calling out, "Hey! It's me! Why am I here? Why am I not at the office? Why are *you* not at the office?"

Russ called out from another room, "Never mind all that. Did you call my dad?"

"Yes," Janet answered. "I told him you'll be there on Sunday to help him move. He almost had a heart attack, if that was your intention."

"What about the plane tickets to Hawaii?" Russ called.

"Booked 'em. Two first-class tickets. You leave at two," Janet replied.

The phone rang. Janet picked it up, then handed it to her boss as he came around the corner. "This is your conference call," she said. Russ reached for the receiver, but Janet held it back, saying, "Wait a minute. You sure you want this call? I mean, you look . . . weird. And you're acting . . . happy. You haven't lost your mind, have you? You do realize what you asked me to do?"

Russ smiled. "I asked you to decide which of our clients are the good guys and which are the bad guys. Then I asked for a conference call with the bad guys." He took the phone from Janet's hand.

"Greetings, everyone," Russ started. "I woke up this morning and realized that, as your own personal image guru, I could make all of your problems disappear with one piece of professional advice. It took me forty years to figure this out, so listen up: *Stop being greedy, selfish, unethical, and deceitful slobs!* Follow that advice, and none of you will ever need my services again. That pretty much wraps it up. Good luck and good-bye."

Russ hung up the phone and looked at Janet, who was standing with her mouth hanging open. She couldn't believe what he had just done.

"Who was on that call, anyway?" Russ asked her.

Janet replied, "Every single one of your clients except Kenny."

Russ nodded. "Ready to start over?" he asked her.

Janet nodded. Then she said, "The full moon

looks orange sometimes when it's rising because the light has to travel through more of the atmosphere than when it's high in the sky. The blue light scatters, but the red makes it through."

"Why are you telling me this?" Russ asked her.

"I don't know," Janet replied, looking confused. "Russel Duritz, are you okay?"

Russ smiled. "Yeah."

Janet handed him the confirmation for his airline tickets to Hawaii. Russ looked it over and scribbled something down on it. "Thanks," he said. "Just change the name on the reservations."

He handed it back to her, and headed out the door.

"Will you be in later?" Janet asked him.

"Maybe. But you won't," called Russ.

Janet looked down at the fax. Russ had crossed out his own name and written in hers. Janet and her husband were going to Hawaii.

Russ pulled to a stop outside Amy's house and got out of his car. Then he reached into the car and lifted out a golden retriever puppy. But this was no ordinary puppy, because it would grow up to be Chester, the world's greatest dog.

Russ stood at the gate of Amy's house. Through the window, he could see her moving around in her kitchen. As he watched, she worked, holding some slides up to the light. She took a sip of coffee, burned her mouth, and silently cursed. A look of utter joy spread across Russ's face as he looked at the woman he was going to marry.

Just then, Amy felt Russ's gaze and looked out the window. Their eyes met. Russ took a deep breath and waited. Amy moved away from the window.

A few seconds later, the front door opened, and Amy stood in the doorway, looking at Russ. The look on her face seemed to say that she knew. She knew everything. Russ took a step forward and made his way up the path, getting closer to his new life with every step.